Shaping Up

2-D Shapes

Suzanne Barchers

Publishing Credits

Dona Herweck Rice, *Editor-in-Chief*; Lee Aucoin, *Creative Director*; Don Tran, *Print Production Manager*; Sara Johnson, *Senior Editor*; Jamey Acosta, *Assistant Editor*; Neri Garcia, *Interior Layout Designer*; Stephanie Reid, *Photo Editor*; Rachelle Cracchiolo, M.A.Ed., *Publisher*

Image Credits

cover Arkady/Shutterstock; p.1 Arkady/Shutterstock; p.4 Cynthia Farmer/Shutterstock; p.5 Charles Shapiro/Shutterstock; p.9 (top left) Edyta Pawlowska/Shutterstock, (top right) Trish/Shutterstock, (bottom) Cheryl Casey/Shutterstock; p.10 (top) R. Gino Santa Maria/Shutterstock, (middle left) Alphacell/Shutterstock, (middle right) Ugorenkov Aleksandr/Shutterstock, (bottom left) Chris Bence/Shutterstock, (bottom right) Nikola Bilic/Shutterstock; p.11 Marymary/Shutterstock; p.13 (top) Cynthia Farmer/Shutterstock, (bottom) Elena Schweitzer/Shutterstock; p.14 Pattie Steib/Shutterstock; p.15 (left) Laurent Renault/Shutterstock, (right) Gordan/Shutterstock; p.17 Dmitriy Shironosov/Shutterstock; p.18 Alexandre Nunes/Dreamstime.com; p.19 Roman Sigaev/Shutterstock; p.21 Moiseev/Shutterstock; p.22 Rob Byron/Shutterstock; p.23 (top) Sean MacD/Shutterstock, (middle) Stanislaff/Shutterstock, (bottom) Tootles/Shutterstock; p.24 R.Filip/Shutterstock; p.25 Nikolay Okhitin/Shutterstock; p.26 Jathys/Shutterstock; p.27 Kristian Sekulic/Margo Harrison/Jacek Chabraszewski/Shutterstock

Teacher Created Materials

5301 Oceanus Drive
Huntington Beach, CA 92649-1030
http://www.tcmpub.com

ISBN 978-1-4333-0424-8

©2011 Teacher Created Materials, Inc.
Printed in China

Table of Contents

Shapes! 4

Circles 8

Triangles 12

Rectangles. 16

Squares 20

Shape Up Lunch 24

Solve the Problem 28

Glossary 30

Index 31

Answer Key. 32

Shapes!

Shapes are all around. Can you find them?

Shapes are even in our classroom.

The teacher says that we will study shapes all week.

We will find shapes. We will count shapes. We will even eat shapes!

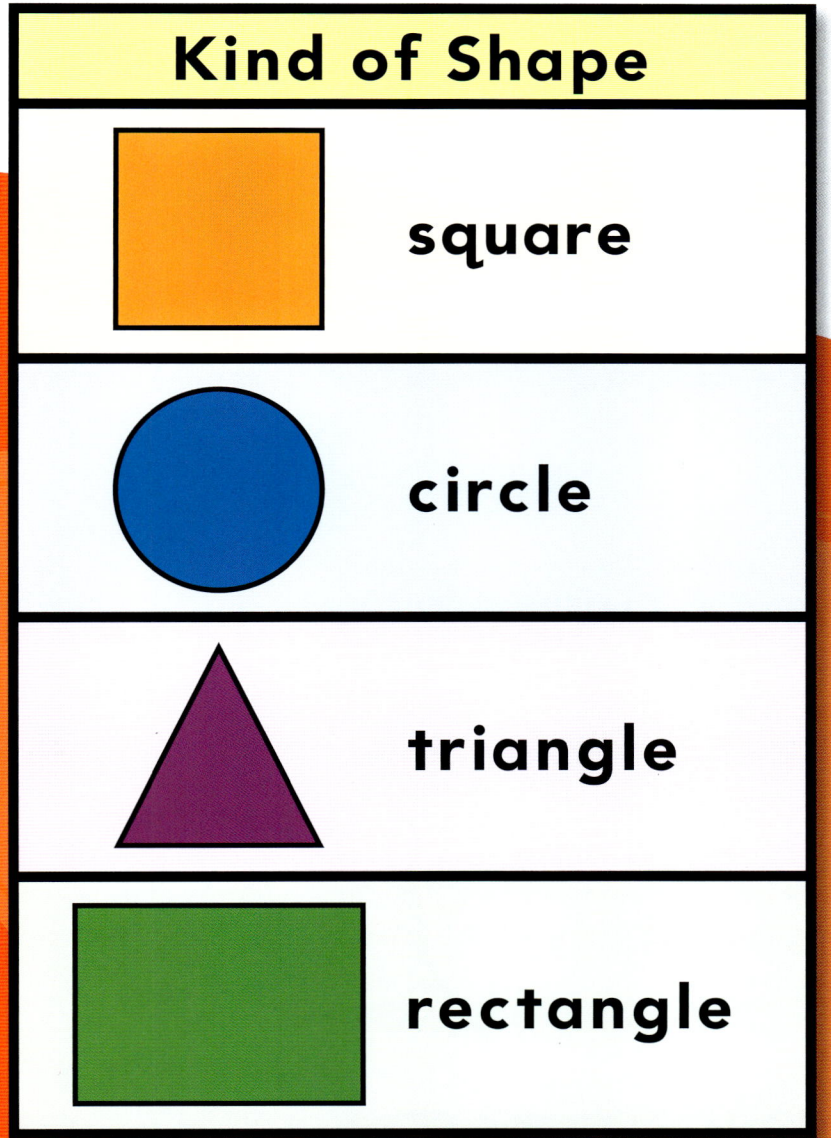

Circles

On Monday, we learn about **circles**. A circle is flat. It is round.

We find big circles first. We see a clock. We see a rug. We also see a table.

We look for small circles next. We see buttons. We see circles on the pencil sharpener.

The class chooses a snack. It must be a circle. Look at the choices. Which snacks are circles?

bananas

crackers

cereal

strawberries

We even find letters with circles!
We make a list of the circles we find.

Circles in Our Room
clock
table
rug
buttons
pencil sharpener
letters O o Q q b d a g p

Triangles

On Tuesday, we learn about **triangles**. Triangles have 3 **sides**. They also have 3 **corners**.

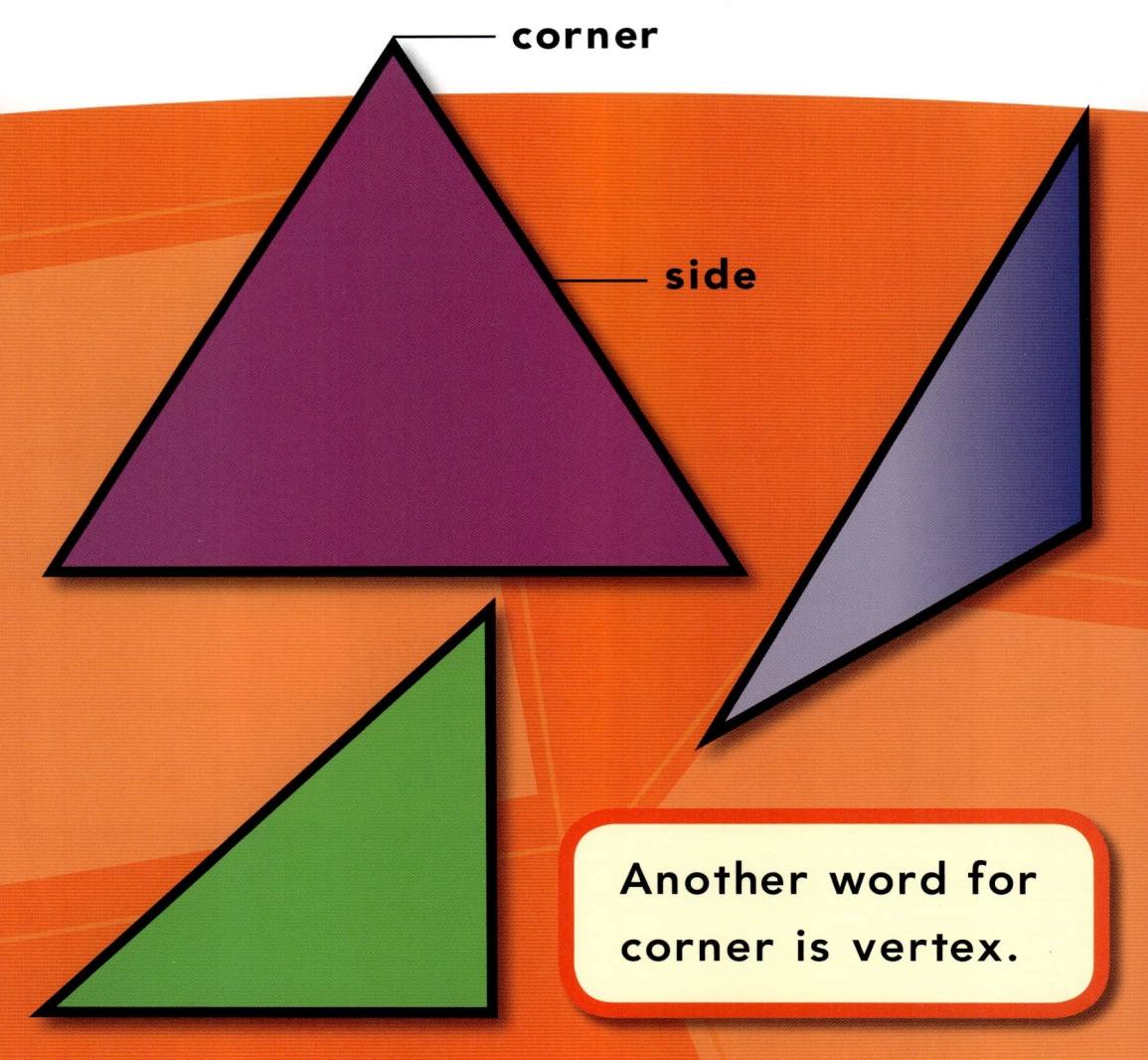

Another word for corner is vertex.

We see triangles on our school.
We see triangles in music class.

We see triangles in books.

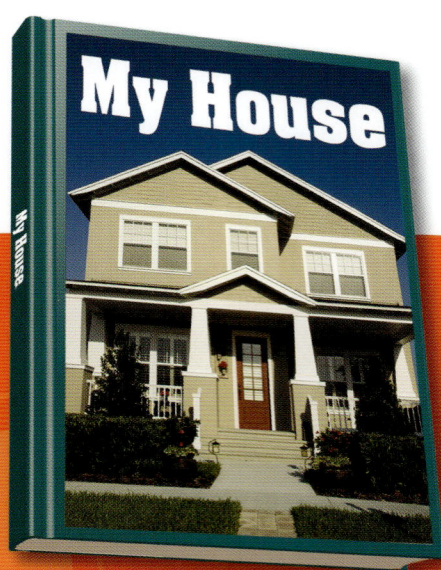

LET'S EXPLORE MATH

These triangles look different.

 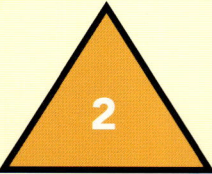 

a. How many sides does triangle 1 have?
b. How many sides does triangle 2 have?
c. How many sides does triangle 3 have?
d. What is the same about all the triangles?

One book has a sailboat.
One book has a tent.

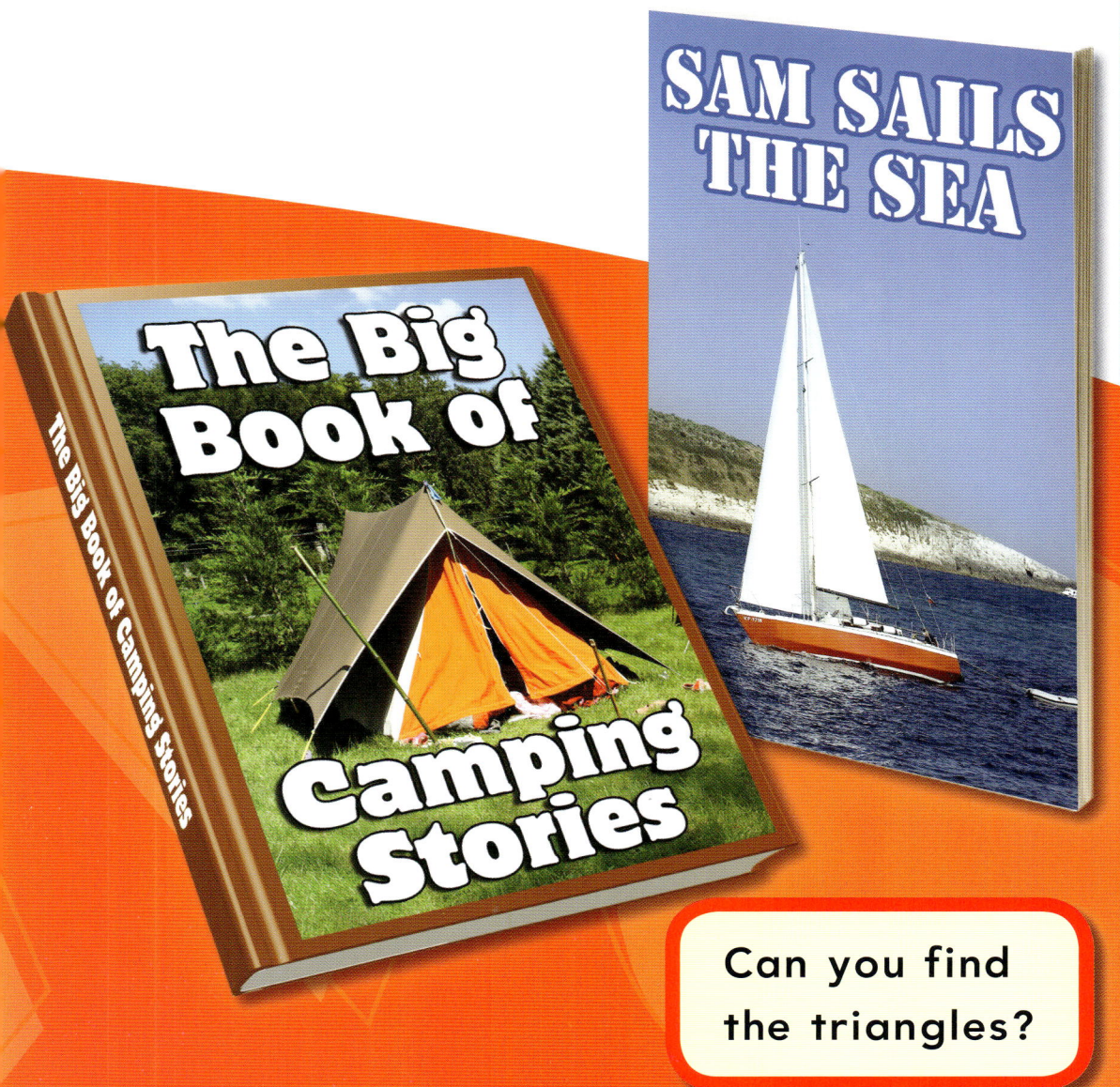

Can you find the triangles?

Rectangles

On Wednesday, we learn about **rectangles**. A rectangle has 4 sides.

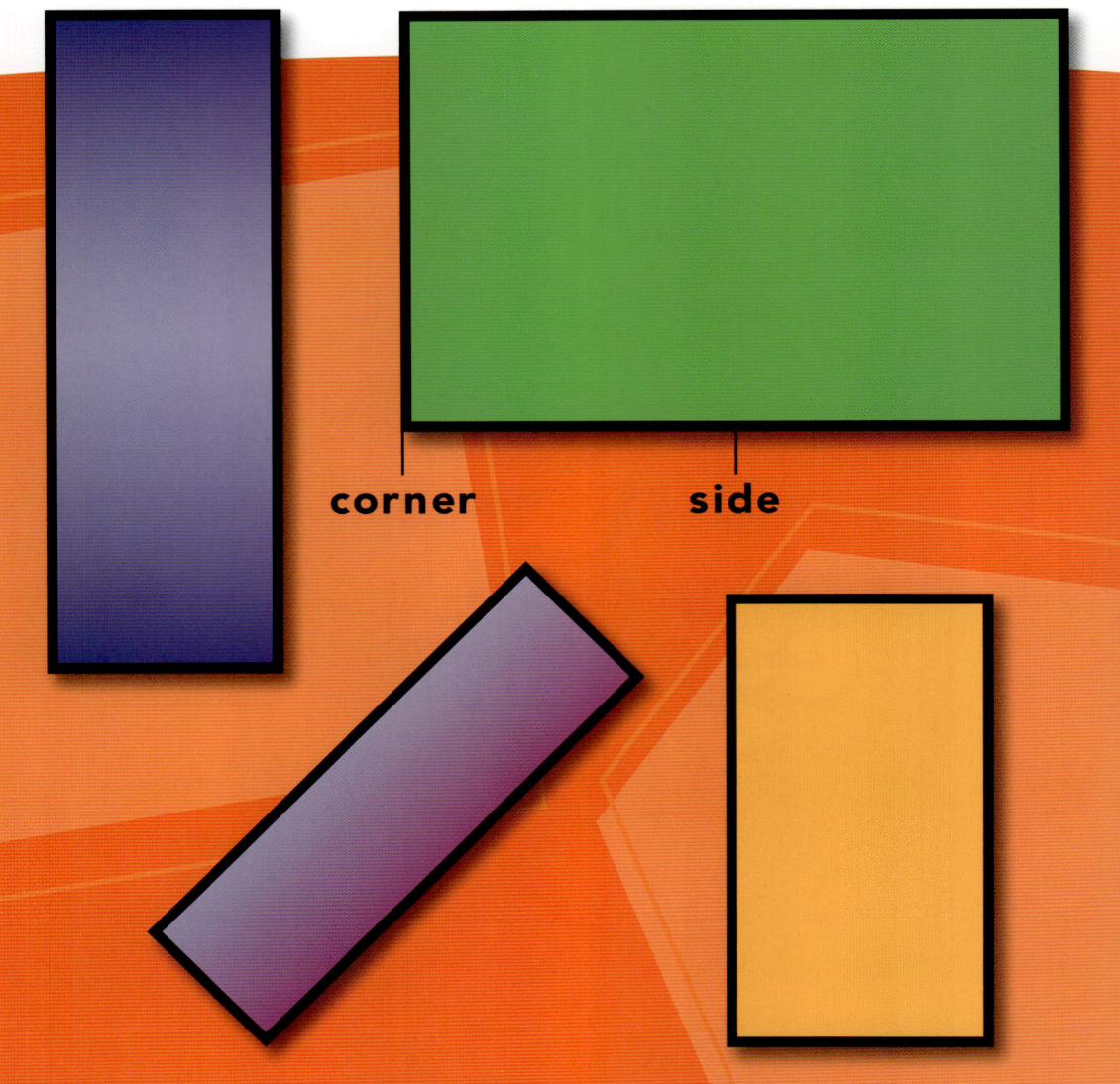

corner side

A rectangle has 4 corners. There are lots of rectangles in our room.

LET'S EXPLORE MATH

The class has a rectangle for snack. How many rectangles can you count in this snack?

We see a bookshelf. We see the board.

We make a list of the rectangles we find.

Rectangles in Our Room
board
desks
windows
bookshelf
books

Squares

On Thursday, we learn about **squares**. Squares have 4 sides. The sides are **equal** length.

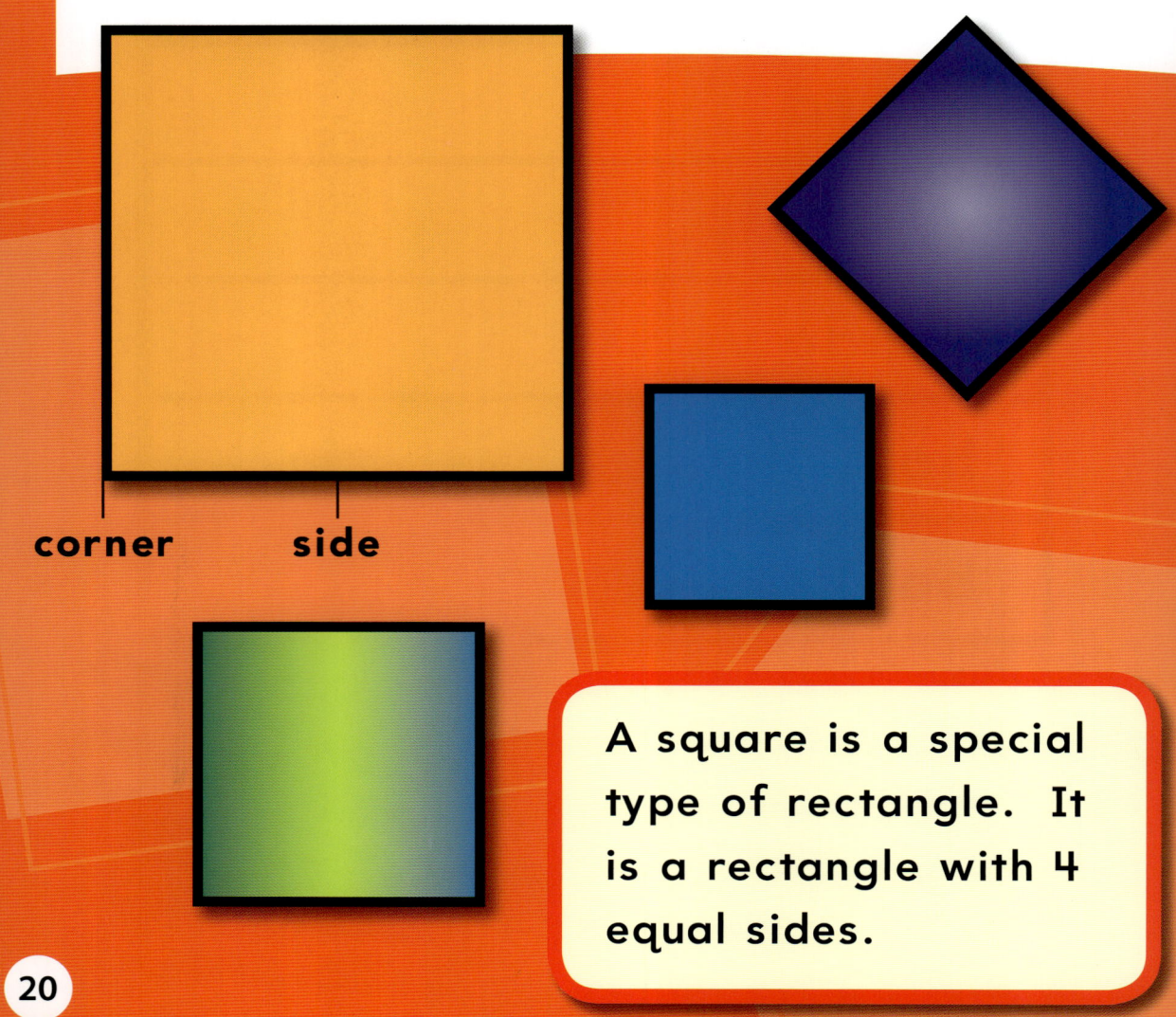

corner   side

A square is a special type of rectangle. It is a rectangle with 4 equal sides.

The keys on the computer keyboard are squares.

LET'S EXPLORE MATH

Look at the shapes.

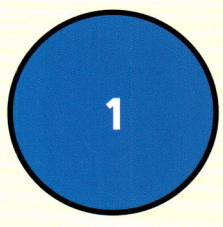   

a. Which shape is a square?

b. Which shape is a rectangle?

c. Which shape is a triangle?

21

We look up and down to find squares.

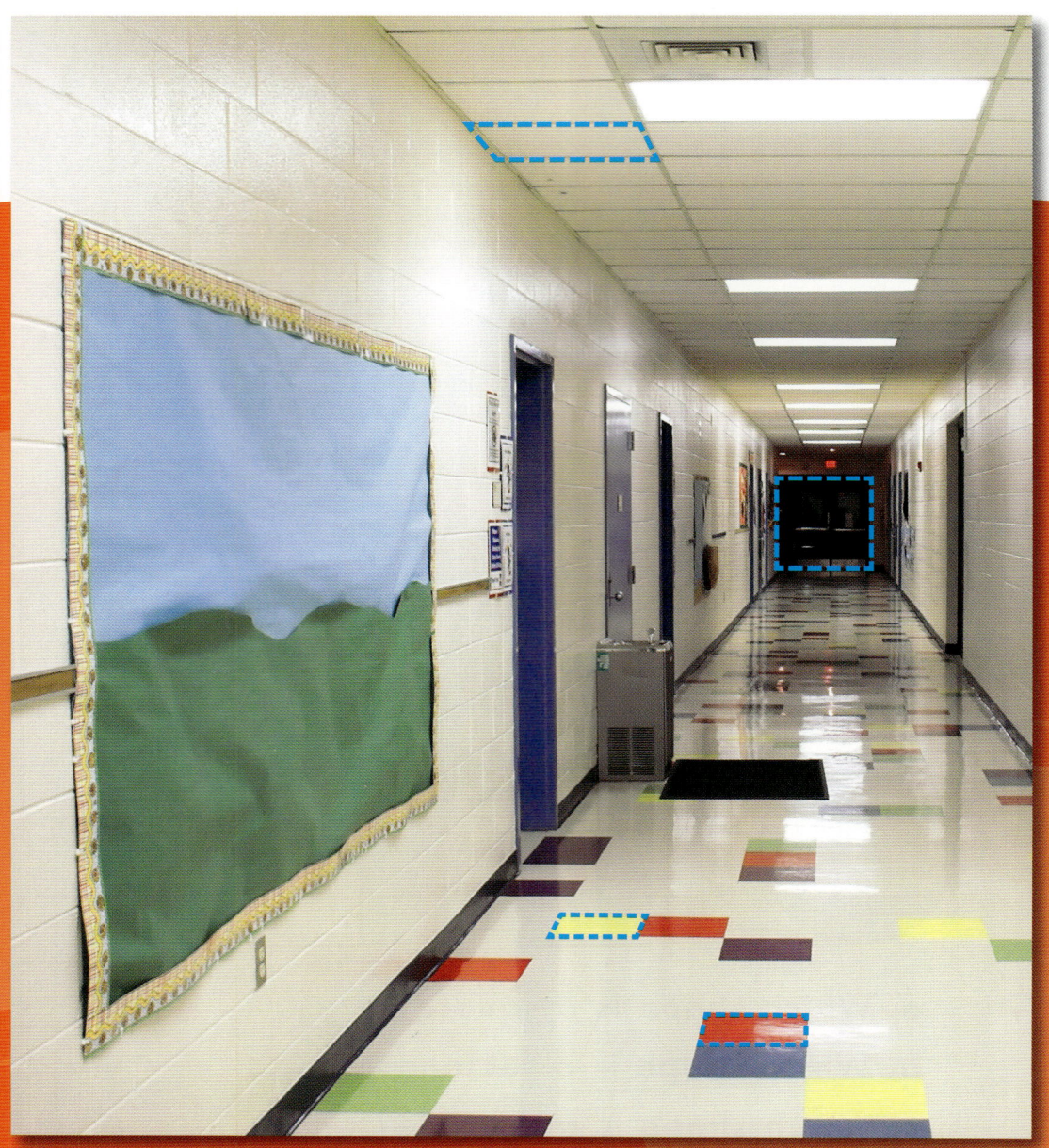

We even voted for our favorite square snack.

Snack	Votes
cereal	9
cheese slices	6
crackers	10

Shape Up Lunch

On Friday, we have a special lunch. The plates are circles. The napkins are squares.

We learn that squares can become triangles if they are cut in half.

A pie starts out as a circle. It looks a lot like triangles when it is sliced.

After lunch, we really try to shape up. Playing with shapes is fun!

Counting Shapes

An artist wants to make the design below. She will use tiles. The design will be used as part of the floor in a museum.

a. How many triangle tiles will she need?

b. How many square tiles will she need?

c. How many tiles will she need altogether?

Solve It!

Use the steps below to help you solve the problem.

Step 1: Look at the design. Count all of the triangle tiles that you see.

Step 2: Look at the design. Count all of the square tiles that you see.

Step 3: Add the number of square tiles and the number of triangle tiles. The sum is how many tiles she needs altogether.

Glossary

circle—flat, round shape

corner—the point where 2 sides meet

equal—having the same amount

rectangle—flat shape with 4 corners and 2 different sets of equal sides

sides—line segments that form shapes

square—flat shape with 4 equal sides and 4 corners

triangle—flat shape with 3 sides and 3 corners

Index

circle, 7–11, 24, 26

corner, 12, 16–17, 20

equal, 20

flat, 8

length, 20

rectangle, 7, 16–17, 19, 20–21

round, 8

side, 12, 14, 16, 20

square, 7, 20–25

triangle, 7, 12–15, 21, 25–26

Answer Key

Let's Explore Math

Page 10:
crackers and cereal

Page 14:
a. 3 sides
b. 3 sides
c. 3 sides
d. All the triangles have 3 sides.

Page 17:
5 (4 small rectangles inside the big rectangle)

Page 21:
a. shape 4
b. shape 3
c. shape 2

Solve the Problem

a. 12 triangle tiles
b. 1 square tile
c. 13 tiles